FLAME
OF
COURAGE
THE CANADIAN FIREFIGHTER

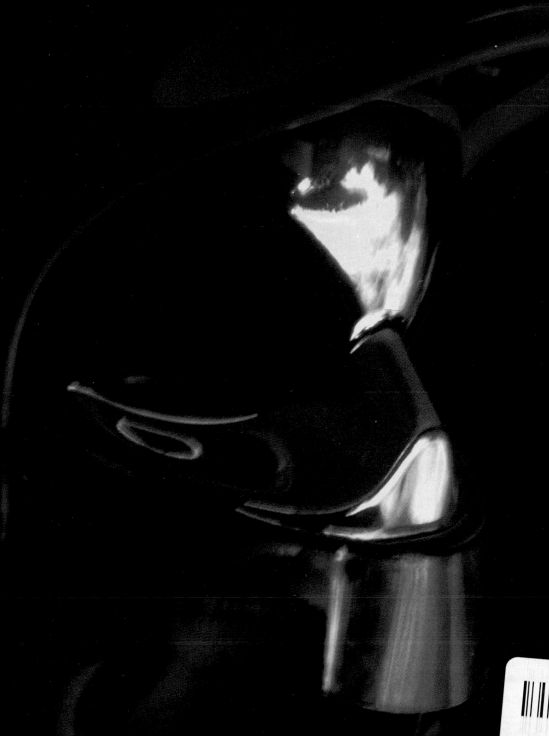

FIREFLY BOOKS

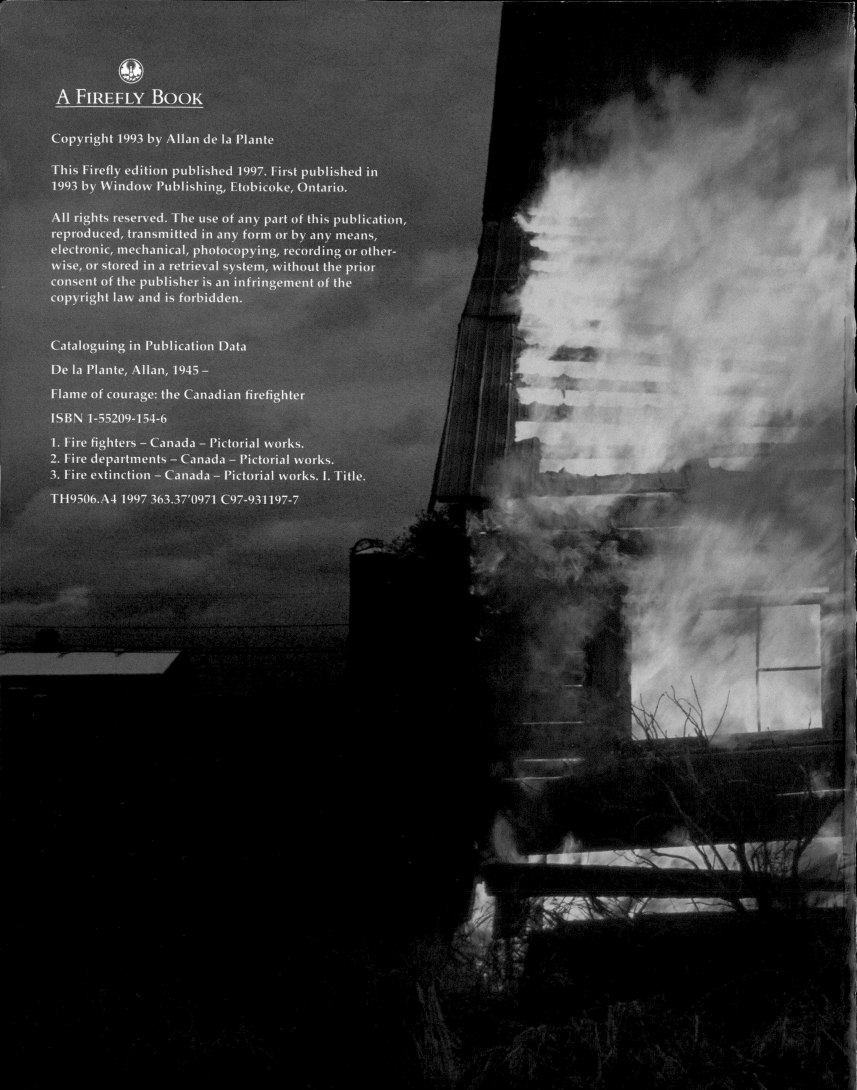

A FIREFLY BOOK

Copyright 1993 by Allan de la Plante

This Firefly edition published 1997. First published in
1993 by Window Publishing, Etobicoke, Ontario.

Cataloguing in Publication Data

De la Plante, Allan, 1945 –

Flame of courage: the Canadian firefighter

ISBN 1-55209-154-6

1. Fire fighters – Canada – Pictorial works.
2. Fire departments – Canada – Pictorial works.
3. Fire extinction – Canada – Pictorial works. I. Title.

TH9506.A4 1997 363.37'0971 C97-931197-7

*To "Red" Bellinger, husband, father, grandfather,
friend and firefighter, whose courage, dedication,
and sense of humour is typical of the Canadian
firefighter ... fight on brother.*

Hey, Alice, this one's for you.

Allan de la Plante

Design and Art Direction: David H. O'Malley, Aerographics
Production: James W. Jones, Alex Moyes, Alain Anka,
Stephanie Owens & Linda Green
Packaging: John McQuarrie, Image House, Ottawa
Colour Separations: Chromascan, Ottawa.

Published by
Firefly Books Ltd. 3680 Victoria Park Avenue, Willowdale,
Ontario Canada M2H 3K1

Published in the U.S. by
Firefly Books (U.S.) Inc. P.O. Box 1338, Ellicott Station,
Buffalo, New York USA. 14205

Printed and bound in Canada by Friesens, Altona, Manitoba

Printed on acid-free paper.

FOREWORD

FLAME OF COURAGE is the definitive book on firefighting in Canada. Only through a pictorial montage can the true essence of the Canadian Firefighter be told. The scope and diversity of the profession is so wide and complex that it would require several volumes of text to even scratch the surface of its responsibilities, so Allan de la Plante took his lead from an old saw which states, "A picture is worth a thousand words".

To graphically capture the firefighter in his milieu, Allan spent six months "living the life" in fire stations from the Atlantic to the Pacific. I had the pleasure of welcoming Allan to my department for one cold week in the winter of '92 on his initial trip across Canada. His enthusiasm for the project was upbeat and infectious, and it occurred to me at the time, that he was displaying the adventurous young man's spirit that is part of the make up of firefighters everywhere. The Allan de la Plante that returned many weeks later was a more reserved person, with a true understanding of the realities of the many tragedies firefighters face daily.

Allan had, now through exposure to the profession, developed the insight to produce a balanced portrayal of Canadian firefighters. This book runs the gamut of the profession through paid, municipal, provincial, federal, armed services, industrial and the backbone of many communities: the volunteers.

As I was privileged to view the hundreds of photographs from which Allan would select, I realized that he had truly captured the soul of the firefighters FLAME OF COURAGE honours, in a very special way, all members of this proud calling.

Barrie J. Lough,
Fire Chief, City of Winnipeg
Director, Fire Prevention Canada

INTRODUCTION

Long before this project ever entered my mind, my idea of a firefighter was some guy in a red truck roaring down the road, kicking in someone's door, making a hell of a mess and going home. This image stuck with me until well into my forties. This all changed while taking portraits of crews and individual firefighters. I found a sensitive, caring group of men and women who put the people they serve well above their own health and welfare. They come from all walks of life, from all levels of society. They all have one goal in mind...to keep you and I out of harm's way.

After being around the fire service about a month, I found myself being drawn into the brotherhood of the firefighter. Their story had been attempted in numerous novels and picture books. I was compelled to tell the story through the eye of the camera. The text comprises conversations and stories from the men and women 'on the job'.

I left my home in Aylmer, outside Ottawa, in late October and drove to the maritimes where I turned tail and headed for the west coast. During the day I drove from one town to another. At night I stayed in the fire halls with the guys, and on several occasions the women, who respond to the call in Canada. I slept in the dorms, slid the poles, and rode the rigs. I ate with them, laughed with them, was the brunt of many a prank, and even pulled the odd one myself. I also experienced the pressure that is part of the life of a firefighter. To me it's one of the greatest jobs. There are, however, many trade-offs for the enjoyment of this profession.

The last thing I expected when I undertook this project was some unseen force that would attempt to destroy my emotional stability. If it were not for the strength of my family and the understanding of the firefighters themselves, I may have come away from this far more scarred.

Of the one hundred and thirty-seven runs as a visitor or 'cling-on', I noticed without exception the dedicated individual striving to maintain a standard on a job that is under constant criticism, mostly from individuals who don't have a clue what this job entails.

It is impossible to describe what it is like to be roused from a half sleep at 3 a.m., having been in your kip for less than twenty minutes. The ride to the call is universally quiet, each man alone with his own thoughts, wondering if this is just another 'bullshit call', or if there is some horror to be burned into the mind long after the rig turns for home. Conversation, if any, relates only to the location of the call.

Most of the calls we answered were of the false variety...the rest were a cross-section of the most brutal experiences I have ever had to endure. To pull up and see four little kids wrapped in blankets sitting on a snowbank just before Christmas as their house burns, or to watch a young girl being cut out of the car that holds the mutilated body of her girlfriend, leaves more than an indelible mark. I had seen many accidents but had never been close enough to hear the sounds of the injured. No actress could duplicate the sound of this young woman. The comfort given this victim was sincere and moving. I tried not to interfere with the privacy of the individuals involved. Her death, when the pressure of the dash that held her together was released, will be forever etched in my mind as I'm sure it will in the mind of the firefighter who held her in his arms.

To them, I offer up this work and hope a little light has been shed on the wonderful, exciting and often brutal life of our most unsung hero, the firefighter.

My one regret is there'll be no excuse to go for a hair-raising ride in the front or rear seat of a pumper or rescue truck. My great adventure with the men and women who live with danger and even death every day they go to work will be over...or will it?

Allan de la Plante
Aylmer, Quebec

THE HALL

"The FIRE HALL is home.
It's where we regroup and pull together
as a family. We laugh and fight and
interact as a unit... just like any family
does. We gather ourselves up after a
call that disturbs us to the core... one
that tears us up inside. It's our safe
place where we can be ourselves
without the prying eyes, without those
who consider us to be something
special... role models. We can bring
each other back to some kind of
normalcy, either through humour,
be it black or not, or through our
Critical Incident Stress teams.

"Open House is a big day for us. We get to meet our neighbours..."

The kids who come to the fire hall are great. Some come with their class or their cub or brownie pack. There are times when you'd like to say "later", but once they are there looking at all the gear and the rigs...it's the look on their faces...you'd think they'd met Michael Jackson. They love to get behind the wheel of one of the trucks and blow the horn. Occasionally we'll get a group where one of the kids' fathers is 'on the job'. He'll strut around, his chest out. It's great to have them visit.

Open House is a big day for us. We get to meet our neighbours, who bring their kids. It's a good opportunity for us to get to know them and they us. It also lets them know that we're not Superman, just regular guys with families of our own.

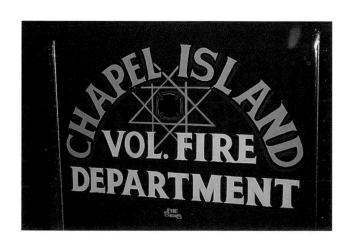

12

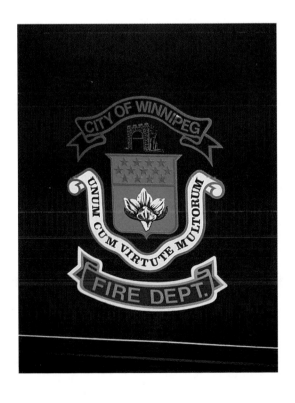

 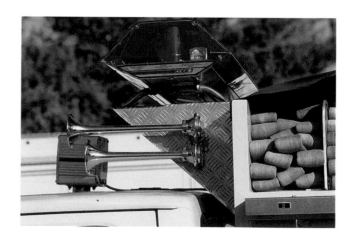

**"To get transferred

to a hall

with a great cook

is a huge bonus."**

Some visitors are surprised to see a kitchen when they get a tour of the hall. Some don't even realize that we don't go home at five o'clock like everybody else. This is our home. We eat, sleep, work out, even go to school here. Some halls have recreational facilities that help us keep in top physical condition. We go to work wherever and whenever we are called. Sometimes the cooks at the hall leave a lot to be desired, but some rival the best in the restaurant business. To get transferred to a hall with a great cook is a huge bonus. If you've got a Ryan, a Veljacic, or any hot cook on your crew, it sure beats call out food."

Learning to cook for eight or twelve is in itself an art. The following recipes are from some of the hottest chefs 'on the job' from coast to coast, so go ahead and see if your 'hot chef' gets the same results from these great feeds.

THE ONLY BBQ SALMON

F/F Dave Veljacic
Vancouver Fire Department
Vancouver, British Columbia

1	salmon fillet (3-4 lb.)(deboned)
10	large garlic cloves (salt mashed)
4	tablespoon parsley (chopped fine)
1/2	tablespoon sun dried tomatoes (minced fine)
1/2	cup olive oil
1	teaspoon salt

With the flat of a wide blade knife crush the garlic cloves, chop them up, pour the salt over the cloves and grind them with the flat of the knife.

Combine the garlic, parsley, sun dried tomatoes and olive oil in a covered jar and allow to sit overnight in your fridge.

With a very sharp knife, cut two lengthwise slits in the salmon fillet, dividing the surface of the fish into thirds. Cut to the skin, but not going through it.

Spread half the garlic mixture over the salmon fillet and into the slits, place on the grill in a gas BBQ at low temperature and close the lid. Cook for 15 minutes.

Spread remaining garlic mixture on the salmon fillet, close the lid and turn the temperature to medium and cook for another 15 minutes, or test the salmon to see if it is done.

Remove salmon from the grill by inserting spatulas between the skin and the flesh of the salmon fillet, lifting the flesh but leaving the skin on the grill. Place the skinless and boneless salmon fillet on a bed of fresh green lettuce.

Serves 6 to 8.

CHICKEN MANDALAY

Acting Lieutenant George Morhun
Winnipeg Fire Department
Winnipeg, Manitoba

4	chicken breasts (deboned)
3	tablespoons flour
1	teaspoon curry powder
1	teaspoon salt

Sauce

2	jars apricot puree baby food (8 oz.)
4	teaspoons vinegar
2	tablespoons honey
1/2	teaspoon salt
1	large onion
1	tablespoon of butter

Combine flour, curry and salt. Cut breasts into 1" strips. Dredge chicken in flour mixture. Brown strips in oil (1/8" each side). Place in roaster. Saute onions in butter. Add vinegar, honey, salt and apricot puree. Simmer for 5 minutes till warm (add water if too thick). Pour mixture over chicken. Cover and bake at 350 degrees for 45 minutes.

Serve with rice pilaff.

TODAY'S CHOWDER

F/F Alphonse Robichaud
Saint John Fire Department
Saint John, New Brunswick

10	potatoes (peeled and quartered)
4	onions (peeled and chopped)
1	celery stalk (chopped)
1	lb. white fish
1	lb. scallops
1	lb. seafood blend
1/2	lb. shrimp
3	lb. clams (in shell)
1	can cream of mushroom soup (19 oz.)
1	lb. butter

Place potatoes, celery and onions in large pot. Cover with water and bring to boil. Add seafood and again bring to boil. Add butter and cream of mushroom soup. Bring to boil. Stir frequently. Serve to the hungry...and even the odd 'cling-on'.

MOOSE STEW WITH BLANKET

F/F Dennis Aylwrad
St. John's Fire Department
St. John's Newfoundland

1/2 lb. salt pork
3-4 lb. moose (cubed)
4   large carrots (cubed)
1   turnip (cubed)
4   large potatoes (cubed)
1   large onion (chopped)
1   teaspoon salt
1   teaspoon pepper
Pastry recipte - see below

In a large roasting pan, render out salt pork. Add moose. Fry till brown. Add onion, salt and pepper. Continue to fry. Add 5 - 6 cups of water after browning. Simmer for approximately one hour. Add cubed vegetables (carrots, turnip, potatoes). Bake for approximately forty minutes in 325 degree oven. Remove from oven and cover with pastry. Continue to bake until brown.

Pastry

2   cups flour
2   teaspoons baking powder
1/2 lb. butter

Mix flour, baking powder and butter in bowl. Add water to moisten. Blend and knead. Roll pastry to baking dish/roasting pan size.

CHICKEN IN PUFF PASTRY
with Mushroom Gravy

F/F Ed Lukachko
Toronto Fire Department
Toronto, Ontario

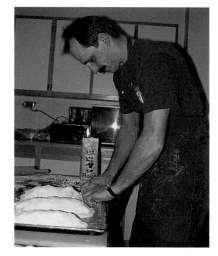

2   pkg. puff pastry
8   full chicken breasts
     (skinless, boneless)
2   cups green onions (chopped)
5   cups cheddar cheese (grated)
2   tablespoons pepper
Egg Whites (for pastry)
Mushroom Gravy - see below

Cut chicken in strips 1/2" wide. Combine with green onions and black pepper. Chill for about 30 minutes. Thaw pastry according to instructions and cut in quarters. Roll out pastry twice as long as it is wide. Place sheets of pastry on baking sheet. Place chicken lengthwise on pastry and top with cheddar cheese. Add second sheet of pastry on top of chicken and cheese. Crimp the edges of the pastry. Brush with egg white and score pastry diagonally.

Bake at 350 degrees for 1 hour and 20 minutes. Serve with mushroom gravy.

Good for 16 servings or 8 in a fire hall.

Mushroom Gravy

2   lb. mushrooms (sliced)
2   medium onions (sliced)
6   tablespoons butter
4   tablespoons flour
2   cups sour cream
2   tablespoons paprika
2   tablespoons salt
1   tablespoon pepper

Melt butter in a large saucepan and add mushrooms and onions. Cook over medium-low heat until tender. Add remaining ingredients and cook over low heat until thick. Stir frequently. Serve over chicken in puff pastry. Also good on toast for lunch.

FRENCH UKRAINIAN PEA SOUP

Captain Ed Kostenko
Winnipeg Fire Department
Winnipeg, Manitoba

3-4   lbs. Ham (with bone) picnic
       shoulder or leftovers
6   cups yellow split peas
1 1/2 cups onion (shredded)
5   qts. water
5   teaspoons chicken bouillon base
1   tablespoon crushed red pepper
1/2   teaspoon black pepper
1/2   lb. bacon (chopped)
1/2   cup shredded carrots

Cut fat and bone from ham. Cube ham. Place ham and bone in soup pot. Add split peas, 1 cup onion (reserving 1/2 cup), carrots, chicken bouillon, crushed red pepper, black pepper and water. Bring to a boil then reduce to simmer. Cover and simmer for approximately 2 hours. Stir occasionally until split peas soften.

In last half hour, remove approximately half of peas from pot, crush and return.

Fry bacon slowly. When bacon is half done, and the remaining 1/2 cup of onion. Fry until brown. Drain. Place on paper towel to absorb excess grease. Add onion and bacon to soup. Let simmer for another 15 minutes.

NOTE: If during cooling soup gets too thick, thin slightly with water.

Serves 4 firefighters or 10 normal people.

CABBAGE ROLLS

Lt. John J. Matlock
Calgary Fire Department
Calgary, Alberta

6	lb. lean ground beef
2	lb. bacon (chopped and cooked)
4	cups Minute Rice
2	medium onions (chopped)
3	medium - large cabbage
3	cans tomato sauce (24 oz.)
1	tablespoon seasoned salt

Microwave each cabbage for 15 minutes (leaves will peel off). Combine all ingredients in large bowl except cabbage leaves and 2 cans of sauce. Extra sauce is to be used as a side sauce. Add 1 tbsp. of seasoned salt. Ball up meat mixture by hand and wrap as tightly as possible in cabbage leaves.
Pack in roasting pan. Cover.
Cook at 325 degrees for 90 minutes.

Serves 12 - 15 hungry firefighters.

PORK BIRDS

Captain Peter Ryan
Ottawa Fire Department
Ottawa, Ontario

8	double butterfly pork chops
8-10	slices day old bread (cubed)
1/2	teaspoon black pepper
1/2	teaspoon savory
1	large onion (minced fine)
2	tablespoons butter
1	tablespoon chicken bouillon base
4	oz. water
Garlic Powder	

Saute onion in butter. In large bowl combine cubed bread, onions, pepper, savory, chicken bouillon and water. Stuff pork chops with mixture. Tie or hold closed with toothpicks. Bake in 375 degree oven for 45 minutes.
Serve with red current sauce and vegetable of your choice.

Red Current Sauce

1	large jar Kraft Red Current Jelly
1	large jar Kraft Crabapple Jelly

Mix red current and crabapple jelly and heat.

Pistachio Pudding with fresh fruit

Captain Peter Ryan
Ottawa Fire Department
Ottawa, Ontario

4 Kiwi
1 pt. Strawberries or Oranges
1 pt. Whipping Cream
2 large pkg. pistacio instant pudding

Prepare pudding according to directions. Top with kiwi and strawberries. Serve with whipping cream.

CHEESE CAKE

Captain Steve Vince
Edmonton Fire Academy
Edmonton, Alberta

Crust

1 1/2 cup Graham Cracker Crumbs
1/2 cup sugar
1 cup butter (melted)

Combine ingredients and flatten in 11" pan. Put in freezer.

Filling

1 1/2 kg. (3 lb.)	cream cheese
1 1/2 cups	sugar
6	eggs
2	teaspoons vanilla
1/2	cup whipping cream
2	tablespoons flour

Beat cream cheese until creamy. Gradually add sugar and eggs, one at a time. Beat on low speed. Add vanilla. Beat for 5 minutes. Blend in whipping cream and flour. Pour over crust. Bake 1 hour at 325 degrees.

Author's Note: This requires two men and a small boy to lift...but the taste!

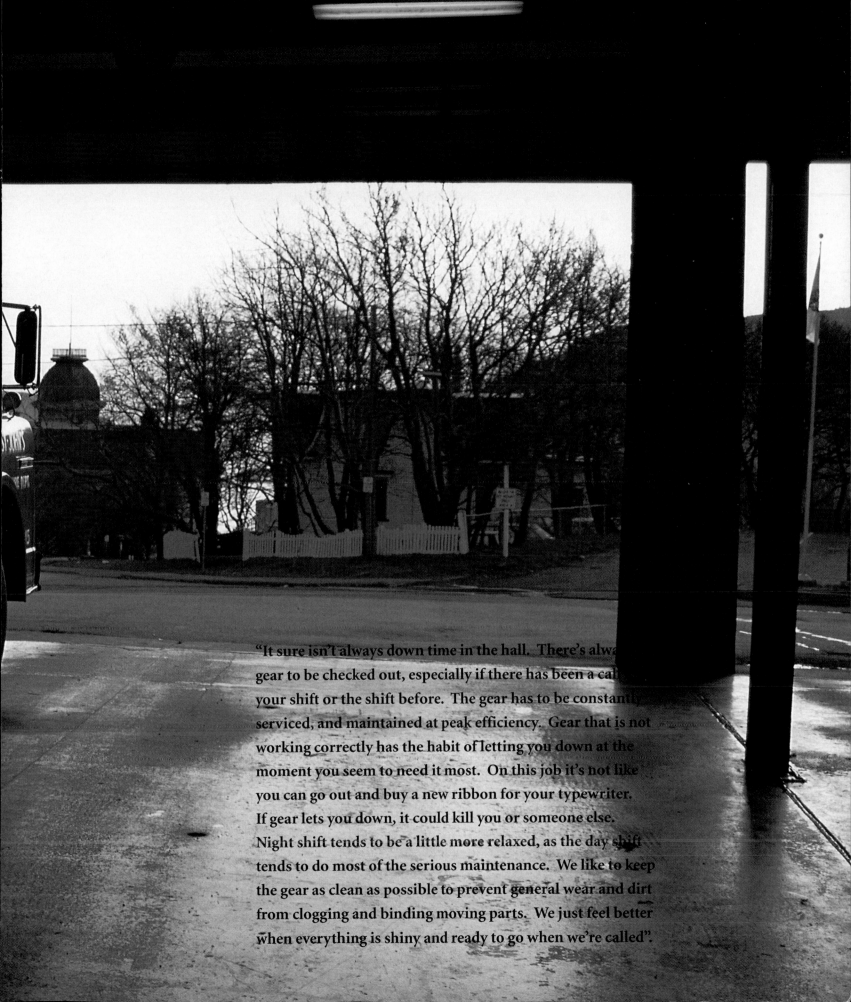

"It sure isn't always down time in the hall. There's alwa[ys]
gear to be checked out, especially if there has been a cal[l]
your shift or the shift before. The gear has to be constan[tly]
serviced, and maintained at peak efficiency. Gear that is not
working correctly has the habit of letting you down at the
moment you seem to need it most. On this job it's not like
you can go out and buy a new ribbon for your typewriter.
If gear lets you down, it could kill you or someone else.
Night shift tends to be a little more relaxed, as the day shift
tends to do most of the serious maintenance. We like to keep
the gear as clean as possible to prevent general wear and dirt
from clogging and binding moving parts. We just feel better
when everything is shiny and ready to go when we're called".

Elsie,
Inch,
Gomer,
Squeeky,
The Brain Surgeon,
Jungle-The-Brute-Tow
The Line,
'Yer a beauty boy',
Swagger,
Big Bird,
Big Red,
Lurch,
Prang,
Boots,
Mother,
Dutchie,
Bomber,
Quiver Lip,
Beaverton,
Poo Bear,
Mr. Dress-up,
Weasle,
Iron Head,
Gerbil Meister,
Tree Pruner,
Casper,
Pancho,
Topper,
Gringo,
The Goat,
Toad,
Corporate Puppet,
Rainbow,
No Neck,
Meathead,

Scarecrow, Gazoo, Waddy, Chip, Homer,

THE CALL

Somewhere in Canada at this very
moment there is a fire burning.
Firefighters will respond to
THE CALL for assistance with the
determination of Olympians.
In protecting the lives and property
of the citizens in their communities,
they will put their own lives on the
line with every response.

**"Can you give me the fire department?
Please hurry!"**

"Just slow down. You have the fire
department. Where are you?"

"Oh, no!"

"Where are you?"

"I'm...uh...I"m...uh, 103 Hartley Road!"

"103 Hartley Road?"

"Please hurry!"

"What's burning?"

"Hurry!"

"What's burning?"

"Pardon?"

"What's burning?"

"Our house! I've got to hang up!"

"We're on our way.
Get out of the house."

ANDERDON
112 114 118
BELLE RIVER
COLCHESTER NORTH
ESSEX
GOSFIELD NORTH
MAIDSTONE
MALDEN
WINDSOR
DEPT
SELECT
CHANNEL 3

"103 Hartley Road, 103 Hartley Road. Engine one, engine three, pump one, car three, rescue one... 103 Hartley Road. Engine one, engine three, pump one, car three, rescue one."

"Engine one responding."

"All units respond to 103 Hartley Road.
The cross street is Midland Avenue.
It's reported as a house fire.
You have a hydrant in front of 111, west side."

"Rescue one responding."

"The caller said it was a fire in the house."

"Fire department."

"You've got a fire at Hartley and Midland."

"Can you tell me what's burning? We have units..."

"It's a house."

"It's a house fire?"

"It's a residence, ya, on the east side of Hartley right at Midland."

"Okay, they're on their way."

"All units responding to 103 Hartley Road.
For your information, we have several calls on this."

"Roger."

"All units responding to 103 Hartley Road.
You have a hydrant in front of 111, the west side.
Also a hydrant in front of 127, the west side."

Hormone, Olf, The Creeper, China Doll, Astral Boy, Hand Job, Shadow, Horsehead, Captain Sleaze,

Red Ass (rookies), Dodger, Buffoon, Low Ball, Swindler, Duck, Deacon, Windy, Jocko, Hushey,

"Engine one come right in with your inch and a half.
The next pump lay into him."

"Message received."

"All units respond to 103 Hartley Road. The cross street
is Midland Avenue. It's reported as a house fire.
You have a hydrant in front of 111, west side."

"Rescue one responding."

"The caller said it was a fire in the house."

"The reason we (dispatchers) are so calm when we get the call is we don't know what's happening at the other end of the line. When the firefighters were answering their own calls, they'd get really excited because they'd been there and seen it. They could visualize what was going on. They'd been there and felt the heat. I've never seen a working fire. I've seen what's left after but I've never felt the heat. I still have a rush of adrenalin but it's just not the same. On some calls, when the caller is in terrible distress, I get a knot in my stomach. It's really hard to remember everything you have to do because you're reacting emotionally to that person's distress. You really have to fight your own emotions to stay calm. My fear is that I might not get the right address. There are so many similar sounding street names. People's accents are sometimes very difficult to understand. If I'm at all concerned whether the address may be incorrect, I play back the tape to review the call. I have to make sure I've sent them to the right address."

An 11 year veteran dispatcher

Hair Ball, Jedo, Monkey, Slim, Hose Nose, Buttsey, Bull, Dapper, Scotty, Beamer, Dinny,

Din Dong, Looner, Wart Hog, Guy Ding, Huck, Mohair, Old Fart, Pin Head, Spider, Granny,

Poon, Dew Drop Dewy, Whitey, Big Bag, Fox Stash, Mr. Green Jeans, Hondo, Grab Bag, Boz,

EMERGENCY
DIAL 911 FIRE
POLICE
AMBULANCE
EMERGENCY

SCOT

T.F.D.

AERIAL
NO. 10

Split End, Goose, Cement Head, Humpy, Gummer, Pretty Boy, Frequent Flier, Top Wop,

When we got there we had a six-door, three-story row, with an apartment on the first floor fully involved.

We were to ventilate and start a primary search. I had a rookie with me

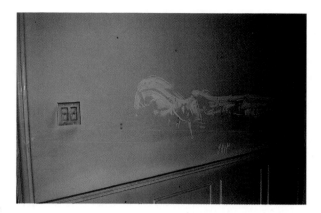

who was at his first fire. It was going to be a wild night for me and 'the kid'. We went into the place next door, past the guys with the lines and upstairs to the apartments. The hallway was full of smoke but there was still no heat. The power had been either cut or burnt out before we got there. We couldn't see a thing. We forced open one of the apartment doors, after checking for heat, and began our search pattern to the right. At one point, something poked inside my mask. I found out the next day that there was a television antenna fully extended inside the apartment. I got my mask sorted out and continued the search. 'The kid' was right on my tail. They lost the first floor but there was still no heat where we were. We couldn't see a damn thing, the smoke was so thick. We found a window with a fire escape. It would be the route home if anything got out of hand. We continued the search and didn't find anything. We couldn't feel it but we could hear it. It was time to bail out. I found a door...it was cool. I opened it and hit a solid wall when I tried to walk through! I couldn't figure out what the hell was going on! There was something seriously wrong! I felt the door from frame to frame. There was a solid wall where the opening should have been! I closed the door and moved further down the wall. I found another door. It was cool so I opened it. Again, I hit a solid wall as I tried to walk through! Where the hell was I? I was totally confused and couldn't find my way out! 'The kid' was still on my ass and mumbling something I couldn't make out. We were both

getting jumpy. We could feel the heat building! It had gone up through the walls and was starting to come down the hallway! Door after door it was the same thing. This went on for five doors! Every time I opened a door, I ran into a wall! The sixth one was hot! We couldn't open it! It was there, ready to greet us with all its fury! We couldn't leave! It was so black we didn't even know where the windows were! The six doors had completely confused me. I knew we were in serious shit and beginning to panic!

I had this kid with me and I figured this was it! We were going to lose it! My ears were starting to pound. It was my bloody heart! It felt like it wanted to crash out of my chest! I was scared shitless and couldn't see a bloody thing! We were finished if we just stood there! I moved again to my left. Through the murk I could see a light. It flashed red-white-red-white-red-white. It was the pump below! I charged the window nearly taking the frame off when I hit it. It was the one with the fire escape. Two guys were bringing up a line on it. I grabbed 'the kid' and pushed him through the window. The two guys on the outside grabbed me by my arms and pulled me out. Back on the ground I pulled off my mask. The air was sweet and cool. That one room had nearly killed us both!

We spent most of the night knocking her down. When it was over I had to go back in to see what had confused me so badly. The room was almost intact. Somebody had taken door frames and doors, painted them all pastel colours and hung them on the wall as decorations! Their bloody art had nearly killed me! I had this kid with me and he didn't even know anything was wrong!

A 27 year veteran firefighter

Gravey Front, Snake, High Pockets, Chummy, Count, I.P.A. Belly, Turkey, Wabbit, Hoss, Frig,

Bugs, Trapper, Bubbles, Weiner, Mr. Everything, Split Ass, Editor, Bubble Nose, Suitcase,

Snork Dork, Ace, Ugly Puss, Rounder, Mug, Alice, Taxi, Turd, Noodles, Mole, Mr. Wonderful,

Studley Do Right, Mac (if you've got it, a trucker brought it) Truck, Popeye, Charcoal Charlie, Tiger,

Rip, Go Go, Pappy, Inky, Slop Chops, Chrome Dome, Worm, Swoop, Jaws, Ann Landers, P.W, Buns

"...I knew they were down there in that hell."

When we pulled up it looked like it would be just a routine call which often turns out to be the worst call...I was driving the Western District Chief. When we talked to the resident he told us he had burned his hand when he was trying to solder an old gas tank in his basement. He said that kitty litter and a few rags he had spread on the floor had just flared up and burned his hands. At that point the chief ordered the pump crew in and the aerial crew to search upstairs and to ventilate. There was just a haze of smoke but nothing great. He told everybody to put their masks on. He couldn't see exactly what was happening. The pump crew advanced 'an inch and a half' into the basement. It was a really cold night. The three firefighters were downstairs for hardly anytime at all when there was a loud explosion. As it turned out the tenant had removed the gas tank from his car with lots of gas still in it. The heat from his soldering, plus the fumes in the tank had started a small fire on the basement floor. He tried unsuccessfully to put it out with kitty litter. Knowing it was hopeless, he ran out the back door. He had closed the door to the basement. He never really explained what had happened downstairs. He just said it was an old tank. We didn't realize it was an old car gas tank that still had gas in it. When the place blew downstairs, the door slammed shut. The Chief kicked the door open to see what was going on. It was just like a torch coming out. The whole stairway was a torch of flame. Shawn had been carrying the tank up the stairs. Enough cold air had gotten down into the basement when they opened the door and advanced the line down the stairs, that we figured the pilot light for the water heater was enough to set off the fumes. Shawn was caught in a 'chimney' going up the stairs! He was totally engulfed in flames! He didn't know where he was. He was able to find the back door and bail out. We didn't see him because he was at the back of the house. Brian and Gary were still down in the basement. One of them had the hose line. He could see the flames dancing all over his body. He turned the line on himself trying to extinguish the fire. He realized it was a lost cause. Meanwhile the other man made a dash up the stairs. The guy with the line booted it up the stairs, as well. We still didn't know where Shawn was. It was total bedlam with everyone screaming for Shawn. They thought he was still inside. There was a lot of panic and upset at that point wondering where Shawn was. Shawn had gone out the back and fallen on the ground. He was still on fire! A lady helped 'put him out'. When he came around the corner, Brian and Gary were crying out for him. We were pouring water on them trying to cool them down. Shawn, even though he was in incredible pain, thought that Brian and Gary were in worse shape than he was. In actual fact, he was the worst of the bunch. He just stood there and said not to worry about him but to take care of Brian and Gary. There wasn't much fire after that. It had burned itself out.

The most traumatic moment for me was standing there when the torch of flame came out the door. I had no line, there was nothing I could do...I knew they were down there in that hell.

A 9 year veteran firefighter

To Hell and Back

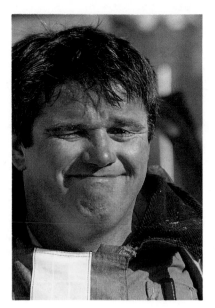

We got to the call and there was smoke showing. This guy came out and said that the kitty litter was on fire. He kept saying "the kitty litter is on fire". He seemed a little strange, and nobody could understand why he was saying that. Somebody told me to grab a pump tank. I grabbed an 'inch and a half' and went down into the basement. Gary and Brian were down there with me. We couldn't find any flame. I was behind Gary on the line. He said he could see a little bit of flame but there was nothing to speak of. There was a lot of smoke. I'm not sure how much time went by but somebody gave me a gas tank and said to take it out. I had it by the filler pipe and under my arm. Unknown to us, the guy had taken the gas tank off of his car. He was trying to fix the gas gauge. He had unsuccessfully tried to empty the gas into a pail. As I was going up the stairs the tank was leaking all over me. THEN THE SHIT HIT THE FAN! I knew something was happening but I couldn't tell what it was. There was so much smoke. I didn't know I was in a 'flashover' or 'backdraft'. My first instinct was to drop the tank over the stairs. At that time I got tunnel vision. Everything...all my systems seemed to shut down. I couldn't hear...everything seemed in slow motion. All the sounds seemed muffled. I just couldn't hear anything. I kept on going up the stairs. The door had been slammed shut by the explosion. The line was jammed in the door. I tried the door, it suddenly opened up. I kept going up toward the kitchen. It was like I had walked into the sunlight. There were flames everywhere. I couldn't see out through the flames. I couldn't see the door. I could see a chair. I picked it up to throw it through a window...if I could find one. There was a break in the flames. It was a doorway. I dropped the chair and ran out the door.

I had run out the back door. There was nobody there except a woman and I think somebody else. The woman started screaming as I came out the door. I was on fire! She was screaming. All I could think about was Gary and Brian behind me ...somewhere...they were still down there! There was nobody around to tell. I didn't know they'd gotten out the front. I still didn't know I was burnt. I didn't know my ears were burnt or my legs were burnt. The woman ran over to me and put something, a coat or whatever, over me. As I was running off the back step, I knew I was on fire. I was ripping everything off and rolling on the ground. She came over and covered me and began to pat out the flames. All I could think about was Gary and Brian. I went to get up but couldn't. I had to spread myself out and get up gradually. I ran around to the front to let them know about Gary and Brian so they could get in and help them. They had gotten out behind me through the front door. They were screaming on the ground. I thought they were worse than I was. Unknown to me, I had been standing right in the 'chimney'. There was no window in the basement. The flames were coming right up the bloody stairs! It was like standing in the middle of a blow torch! In the ambulance they were pouring saline solution over my legs but all I could think about was a picture I had seen the year before in Canadian Firefighter of a guy that had his ear burnt off. I kept asking the attendant about my ears. I kept asking him because I didn't believe him. All I could think was that I didn't have any ears left. I knew they were burnt but I didn't know how badly.

My family went through more than I did until I really started to recover. I was out of the hospital in seventeen days but I was far from recovered. I had gone to HELL AND BACK.

Time is the biggest healer. My wife and I had some difficulties but she's the strongest woman I know. She was my pillar of strength. I couldn't do the basic things in life. She got me through it.

Going back inside was tough for me. I had a

lot of sleep disturbances for the first year. I couldn't concentrate. As a firefighter you're always exposed to human tragedy. We just like to help people...even if it's to get a cat out of a tree.

When I was debriefed it was like a great load was taken off my shoulders...just talking about what happened. It helped to be able to relive it and peal away the layers of hurt. I didn't realize that I was still carrying around the impressions of my first big fire just after I started the job. It was an arson fire down on Kent Street. It killed two kids. I can still smell the burning flesh but I carried around the emotional hurt for years. Just talking about it would have relieved a lot of the stress and hurt that I carried. When I was debriefed about my recent incident, all the extra baggage I was carrying around came to the surface. I had suppressed it. It still was there, hurting whenever my mind strayed or was triggered by something from the past.

I didn't know what to think when Wayne (Corneil) came into my hospital room. I thought he was just lost and looking for directions. When he told me who he was and what his background was and that he had also been a firefighter, I felt comfortable that he would understand. That's why most of the people who are on our debriefing teams are 'on the job'. They understand. They've been there...they know you're hurting.

When I got back to work the support was total. That, I'm sure, helped speed my recovery.

I sympathize with the 'volunteers' now. I probably didn't even think much about them. Those guys...when they get a call, they get an address that comes over their pager. Most of them put a house to that address. I suppose many of them can put a name to that house. I wouldn't doubt that quite a number can even put a face to that name. They will be so charged by the time they get there...it's someone they know. Whether they like them or not, it's someone they've dealt with and have had some kind of relationship with. It has so much greater toll on you emotionally when you know the victim. Even if it's only something minor and nobody gets hurt. You hate to see them in their personal tragedy, no matter how big or small.

The worst is when there are kids involved. Kids really chew you up inside.

The Critical Incident Stress teams that are now beginning to be a regular part of debriefing are helping us to understand what has happened to us emotionally, and to cope with these feelings.

A 16 year veteran firefighter

The Zoo Keeper, Buck, Preacher, Lucy, Rivet, Arab, Flunky, Bingo, Wimpy, Mickey, Sluggo,

Dubber, Ape Head, Bunk Bed, Pipe Neck, Pudgy, Wart Ass, Diggs, Poppa Smurf, Tattoo, Jelly, Stool,

When a building burns, many things happen at once, and most are terrifying. 'The fear,' writes reporter Jeff Lee, 'was indescribable.'

Officially, it was Incident No. F9240153. It started at 8:12:43 p.m. on Nov. 8, 1992. By the time it officially ended the next day, two people were dead, 12 were hurt and a woman was charged with manslaughter.

This is the transcript of the second of two phone calls that came in from occupants at 1356 Franklin. The first, was logged by fire dispatchers at 8:12:43 p.m. This one, from an unidentified boy in the upstairs apartment, was recorded at about 8:15 p.m. The boy dropped the phone as soon as Dispatcher John Hudson told him to get out of the building. The dispatchers could then only hear screams, some words and the sirens of Capt. John Katanchik's pumper as it crossed East Hastings at Clark.

Hudson: "Fire department."
Boy: "Yeah, we have a fire here."
Hudson: "What's your address?"
Boy: "1356 Franklin Street."
Hudson: "1356 Franklin Street?"
Boy: "Yeah."
Hudson: "What is burning there?"
Boy: "What?"
Hudson: "What's burning?"
Boy: "I don't know. I think it's downstairs."
Hudson: "It's downstairs?"
Man's voice in background: "Everybody get out!"
Hudson: "Maybe you'd better get out of the building, then."
The boy drops the phone, and Hudson can only listen to voices in the background as the fire takes hold. While the father drags one child down the stairs and out the front past the fire, the mother tried to get the rest to climb on the roof of the porch.

Woman: "Get the baby, get the baby. Get the kids."
Second female voice: "Where the hell's the baby?"
Man's voice: "Clear out the house!"
A boy's voice: "Where the hell's the baby?"
Woman's voice: "What's happening? Get the baby."
A boy's voice: "She's not in the room!"

Woman's squealing voice: "Ohh..."
Child's voice: "It hurts..."
Screams and squeals.
Hudson's voice comes back on the line.
Hudson: "Hello? I think they're gone."
But the line stays open, and there is more crying and screaming.
Man's voice: "Come on, come on."
Unidentified female or children's voice: "I can't get past the fire to get outside."
The woman tries to get her children to jump out the front window.
Woman: "Get up. Get up here."
A child screams in pain.
Tiny baby coughs.
Woman, in a high-pitched scream: "Up, dammit. On the roof."
Screams and wails.
Child's voice: "I can't get up!"
Woman's voice: "What the f—- is going on. Get up the god-damned drainpipe."
She says something else unintelligible.
Child: "I'm here, and the baby, mom. And the baby."
Woman: Where's the baby...oh, my God."
More screams are heard, and a baby starts screeching.
Sirens from Capt. John Katanchik's pumper can now be heard a block away at Clark and Hastings.
More screams. Now the smoke is so thick that the children are starting to choke and cough, and the baby screeches again.
A boy chokes out: "I can't f——— breathe, man. Help me. I can't breathe. I can't breathe. What the f—- is going on..."
Hudson breaks in: "Nobody answering on the phone there but you can hear something burning in the background."

The screaming reaches a fever pitch as the line goes dead.

For two days I have searched for the words to start this story. With all the scenes of fire and blackness and bloated and burned bodies locked in my mind, the words do not come easy.

How can I begin to explain the horror and abject fear I felt as I entered the blackened, smoking remains of that building, looking for the bodies we all knew would be there?

How can I tell you what it was like to stumble up a dark, debris-filled staircase, a black rain of ash-filled water spraying down upon me, cold water spraying down upon me, cold water flooding into my boots, and acrid black smoke buffeting my masked face?

A body on bed and the sounds of a house dying

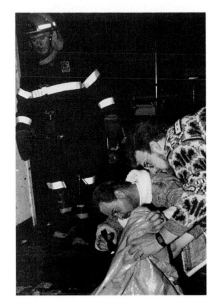

Turning a corner, I saw through the gloom of the smoke a curtain of dripping tar aflame, zip-zip-zipping into the ash and water in which I stood ankle-deep.

Ahead of me, firefighter Randy Olsen had pushed deep into the house with a floodlight, and we were suddenly plunged into even deeper blackness when the extension cord popped out of its socket back at the fire engine. The two of us, alone, in this wreck of a burning building...oh God, the fear was indescribable.

And the heat. That incredible, intense furnace that radiated from every wall as if someone with a flamethrower stood on the other side, blasting me into a deep sweat. I silently thanked God for my protective jacket and the Scott air pack which noisily gave me life at the end of a mouthpiece.

Can I describe the sound a wooden house makes when it is dying? The crackling of flames is nothing compared to the roar of the tonnes of water cascading into it, pouring into every corner and gushing down the stairs and out every possible orifice.

This four-apartment rooming house creaked and groaned around me with the weight of the water as pieces of roof collapsed inward with a crash. Yet the fire raged on in little hot spots everywhere.

And the bodies...the moment when Battalion Chief Syd Duncan swept his light across the downstairs room illuminating the corpse of the man lying face-up on the bed. The arms on the hairless, clothesless body were locked in an L-shape because the heat had tightened his muscles, and his mouth was wide open as if locked in one last horrific scream.

Can I tell you about the surreal scene upstairs, after the fire had been knocked back even further? The six of us, in what was left of the upstairs living room, stared at what appeared to be a piece of sodden foam in the middle of the floor. The moon shone through the gaping roof, which was ringed with smoke and still dripped fire, and our boots squished and squelched in the deep water.

We all knew what we were staring at, but no firefighter could bring himself to lift it to confirm to his bosses that this fire had claimed yet another life. I would later find out that this was an 11-year-old boy, nearly the same age as my oldest son, who was at home sleeping safely in his bed.

I stumbled back down the stairs, dragging deeply on the air, trying to get a grip on what I'd seen. Tears flooded my eyes, and they weren't from the smoke.

Duncan peered at me anxiously, and asked me if I was all right. I passed it off with a brave smile and nonchalant response, and hoped that he hadn't seen me crying.

To an observer, this was horror and fear at their apogee, and I suppose one could be faulted for speaking so graphically of them. What I saw and felt in one brief night is what all firefighters expect to encounter daily in their hard and dangerous lives.

And if, in a few short words, I must tell you what they must face day in, day out, can you understand why these words are so hard to write?

Anyone who is not affected by these scenes is an automaton. No firefighter I saw that night was an automaton.

Later, after most of the 38 men who fought that fire had gone back to their halls, those who were most directly affected gathered with their critical incident stress teams to spill their guts.

I wish that I had been included. Those scenes are etched in my mind. They are brought back to life every time a fire truck passes by.

In time, perhaps they will fade. But this new awe I have for these firefighters will not.

Jeff Lee, Reporter
The Vancouver Sun

Pillsbury Dough Boy, Tim Horton, Blinky, It's Slippery Out Tonight, Twitch, Ref, Wet Back, The Token,

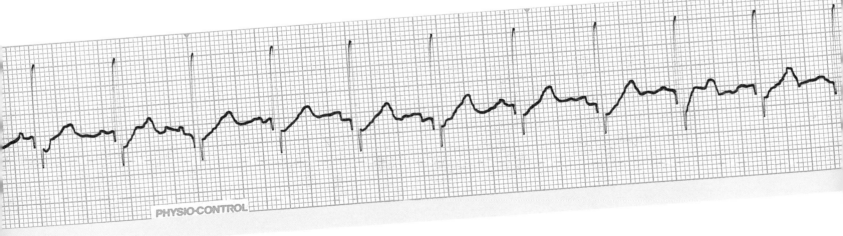

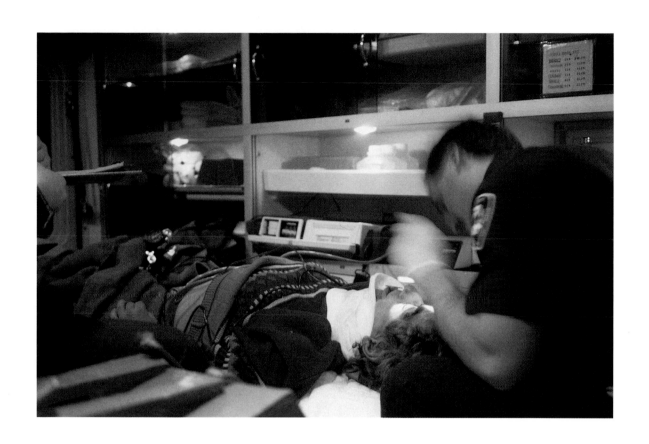

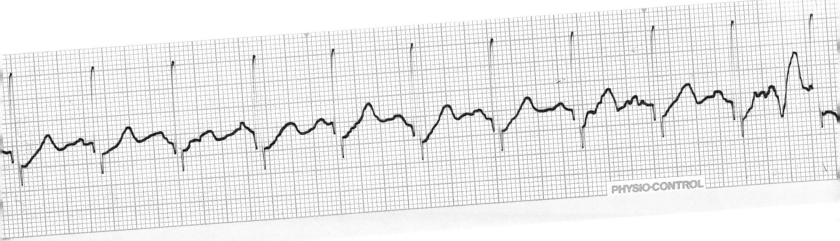

THE VICTIMS & THE FALLEN

Firefighters never go down easily. They go down fighting, cursing themselves for failing to retrace the series of 'rights', or hearing their warning bell over the noise and excitement of even the most insignificant-appearing call.

Their newest and deadliest foe is the one
that eats away from the inside while all seems
normal. The vapours and fumes from chemical
fires and spills, coupled with many synthetic
materials, smoulding their noxious poisons.

"Once we've got her knocked down, I can't
wait to get that damned mask off. Your eyes
burn like hell...but they always do."

Meanwhile the unseen killer stalks its prey.

———

"There's no way to monitor what we go
through. It's like a woman saying that child
birth is hard. I can't relate to that. I can say that
I can imagine that it's hard but I can't conceive
what it may be like. I can't imagine being an
amputee. I can't think of being in a wheelchair
for the rest of my life. You can't imagine what
it's like being inside a fire, thinking and
knowing, that you've got about ten more
minutes of air and you're not really quite sure
where you are. You couldn't know what that's
like unless you've been there. You know if you
don't get your ass out of there and fast, you're
history. Nobody can help you but the man
upstairs and you yourself."

Laughter, most of it brought on by pranks or black humour, becomes the 'safety valve' that helps them cope with the tragic and brutal situations that firefighters must face, often on a daily basis.

Every hall seems to have a court jester or two who are called upon to created laughter, when laughter is the best and sometimes the only medicine available. Through the sharing of humour, firefighters transcend the tragic, to a healthier state of mind and spirit.

Critical Incident Stress teams now debrief the crews that have been exposed to incidents most likely to have adverse effects on them.

Firefirghters experience similar stress levels as Vietnam veterans. They are as stressed out as any of the men who saw combat. The difference is, these guys go back through it over and over again. The longest anyone spent in Vietnam was four years. Firefighters spend thirty to thirty-five years in their careers...if they last that long.

"Firefighters experience similar stress levels as Vietnam veterans"

They are responding to medical and hazardous material calls more than they are to fires. These are the types of call that really disturb them. They have to deal with suicides, and people in a lot of pain and misery. There isn't a lot they can do except give a little comfort. Many of these people just don't make it. It's nice to watch "Rescue 911" where every type of incident happens. Then along comes 'the white knight on his trusty steed' and everyone goes home and lives happily ever after. That's just not how it really is. The guys return from most medical calls and say "...at least we tried but it sure as hell doesn't feel good".

The big myth on this job is "...I don't take it home with me". They get out of the car and head toward the house like Godzilla toward Tokyo. Their families don't know that they've been upset by something. It's not long before they know there is something wrong but they don't realize it is a lot deeper than just a tiff with the boss at work, or some driver that cut them off on the way home.

The other classic is the guy who comes home, dumps on his wife and feels better while she sits there stupefied by what's been said.

Black humour is one of the saving graces. It's one of the things that keeps them alive. It's the thing that keeps them sane. With it, they are able to put some distance between themselves and whatever it was that disturbed them.

Firefighters are not insensitive people. What they've had to do is develop a shell to protect themselves from their own feelings. That's what ends up hurting them. When they are on the fire ground or the scene of an accident, they don't have time for emotions. When all settles and their emotions start to come to the surface, many will say to themselves '...I don't like these feelings', and suppress them. Struggling with these emotions takes tremendous energy.

Dr. Wayne Corneil, MSW Sc. D.
Post Traumatic Stress Disorder Consultant
School of Medicine
University of Ottawa

Doody, Hulkster, No Donuts Boyd, Yuppie, Bozo McTrout, Lt. Pain-in-the-arse, Soupy, Thumper,

140

Mother Goose, Taz, Winky, Sampan, Stop Sign, Hookie, Wayne de Wolfe, Shiney Joe, Crazy Horse,

145

First, we try to determine the origin area of the fire. We check the perimeter of the fire to try to key into the center of origin through burn patterns that tell us the fire started here and extended over there. From this we can determine, for example, that the fire started in the kitchen by the burn patterns and the depth of char. Then we concentrate on that area to try to determine what caused the fire. It could have been an electric heater, a pot of grease left on the stove or that someone poured gasoline there and set a fire which killed two people and injured a firefighter. We're very concerned about that. It is our intention to find out whether or not it was arson.

We have a German Shepherd named Smoke who's trained in cause detection. He's trained through the use of tennis balls with various accelerants on them. In his mind he's having fun. While he is hunting for his tennis ball, he is working for us. He thinks he's in there fetching his ball. He barks and scratches and growls at the area in the fire debris where he thinks his ball

is. We take a sample, have it examined by the lab and low and behold there's gasoline or some other accelerant in the sample. His reward, of course, is a tennis ball. He's trained on twenty-two different accelerants. The tennis ball we reward him with is just an old ball we throw to him when he indicates where there is an accelerant.

Arsonists primarily use gasoline. They also use paint thinner. They use products that are readily available to the layman. You can stop at any gas station and buy a gallon or two of gas. Similarly, you can stop in at a hardware store and pick up a can of paint thinner, varsol or lacquer thinner. In most cases some of this liquid will migrate and get trapped where it can't evaporate or fuel the fire. It's that remaining residue that Smoke can identify.

Richard (Dick) Walters
Fire Investigator
Origin & Cause Inc.

ORIGIN AND CAUSE

153

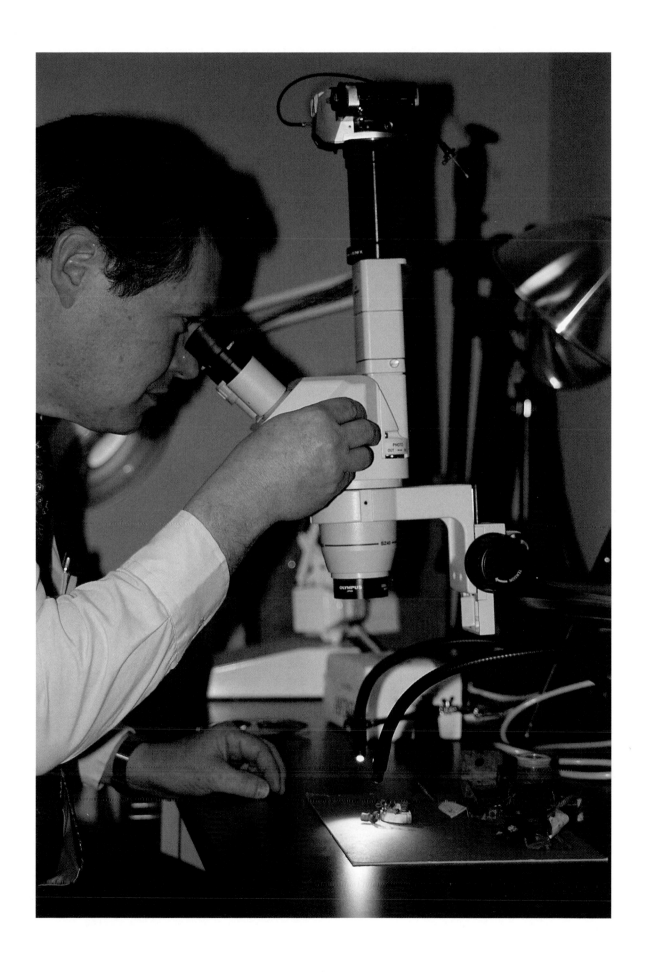

FOREST FIRE

WITH A LITTLE HELP FROM MY FRIENDS

KUWAIT ABLAZE

The Middle East has been a hotbed of ethnic conflict since modern man began to record history. During the 1980s the power-hungry were hard at work. This work would have impact on the world, and the Canadian firefighting community.

Iraq, led by Saddam Hussien, invaded Kuwait and brought the world to the brink of a world war. A united force of world military power crushed the aggressor and pushed his armies in defeat back into Iraq. During their retreat, the Iraqis severely damaged or set KUWAIT ABLAZE with 732 oil wells, creating the largest oil field emergency in history. Ten different countries fought these fires and controlled the spread of impending ecological disaster. In eight months, Canadian firefighters tamed more blazing oil wells than any other country. Some of the largest and most challenging wells were tackled by the small Canadian crew, which brought respect from the established oil field emergency crews.

Hot gas fires will burn at 4000 degrees. It was between one hundred and one hundred and forty degrees in the shade...if you could find any. This was without the fires. The air temperature near the fires ranged from eight hundred to fifteen hundred degrees.

In many cases we had to build a road across an oil lake with sand, just to get to some of the well heads.

At some of these well heads, there was a build up of coke residue twenty to twenty-five feet high and sixty feet in diameter. This mountain of residue hid the source of the fire. We had to claw all that stuff away before we could fight the fire.

There were three aspects to our job in Kuwait. Putting the fire out, killing the well, and then capping it.

Some of the scenes were so compelling that one became confused about what beauty really means.

At times, the oil just rained down from the sky.

Nobody knew how tough it was going to be or how long it would take. Some of the estimates ranged as long as ten years. This project made novices of experts.

We were the new kids on the block. We had everything to prove and nothing to lose. We were up at three in the morning and worked until dark, although it was sometimes dark all day due to the smoke and oil rains.

When we first got there the Americans wouldn't even talk to us. They would barely look at us. You could cut the tension with a knife. We soon showed that we could cut the mustard, and the attitude changed.

I sometimes sit and can't believe that I was there. It just seems so far away and now it's just so cool...it was like hell on earth."

Paul-Emile Ouellette
Canadian Firefighter in Kuwait

"Canadian firefighters tamed more blazing oil wells than any other country"

TEACH FIRE PREVENTION TO SOMEONE YOU LOVE

"Kids don't want to be told what not to do. They want to be told what to do. They want direction. So we tell them to TEACH FIRE PREVENTION TO SOMEONE YOU LOVE."

Getting the message to them when they are young and impressionable, and regularly reinforcing it with our programs as they grow up, creates such an awareness on their part, that each one of them becomes a 'fire prevention officer' in their own home, office or job site."

"If you can sell the idea to the kids then they'll sell it to their parents. If they believe in you, they go home and do their homework. It's the same as when they want a

"If you can sell the idea to the kids then they'll sell it to their parents."

bike. They keep after their parents about when they can go and look at the bikes. They get the catalogues out and keep at it until their parents get the message. It's almost as though the parents say 'let's get it over with', so they can get

back to the job of running the family. If we've sold the kid on the idea of fire prevention, he'll keep after his parents until he gets the same result as in the quest for the bike. The fire prevention message we can get to the kids but it's nearly impossible to get through to the adults.

We try to reinforce our programs through repetition at least three or four times a year. This seems to let everyone know that we really care and don't want to have to make any unexpected calls to their house.

Various projects created by firefighters, help to create public awareness about firefighting and fire prevention in the community. Participation in parades, snowsuit funds, and appeals to help the less fortunate, increase the visibility of the fire service. We tend to support not only those who have been affected by fire or some related incident, but also those who are in need.

Many of the projects we have are aimed at kids. Collecting old fire trucks and restoring them to better than original condition, dramatically illustrates the progress from simple vehicles and equipment of yesteryear to high performance teams that protect the lives and property of people...those from the smallest of villages with a dozen or so volunteers to the massive city forces."

Don Moreau, Directeur
Edmunston Fire Department
Edmunston, New Brunswick

 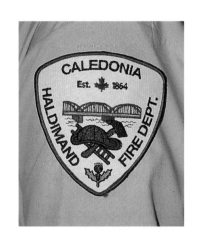 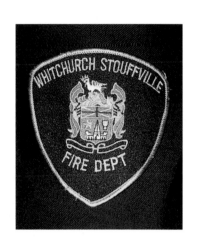

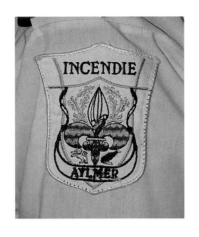  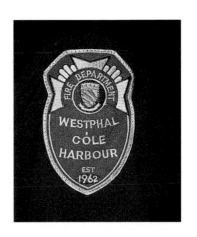

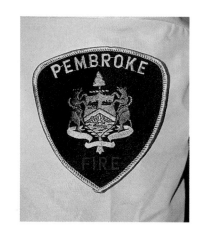

...ONLY ONE GUY THINKS HE DOES IT BETTER!

About the photography

It didn't take me long to realize it would be impossible for me to get the exciting type of photography for a book of any quality by myself. I started to put out the word to the guys on the job and found some of the most remarkable sources of material. Much of it comes right from the firefighters themselves. Many of the pictures herein are taken by off duty firefighters or staff photographers. A husband-wife combo in the west that shoots everything from fires to horses to calender boys, to a wild haired kid who has a scanner and rides his bicycle to record his heroes on film. Professional photographers and people in the community who just happen to be there and got that elusive shot are all represented. Most remarkable of the lot was a young man who roams the streets of the Montreal area with several scanners tuned into different dispatchers. His work is in such demand from firefighters and other officials that he no longer pursues his original profession of carpentry. The quality was something we could not compromise and I am sure you will agree we have the best of the best.

Photo Credits

Saskatoon F.D. Jim Dubois, Tim Walts, Brian Smith,
Greg Sayer 2 - 3, 176T
Jim Kerr 17-MR, 56, 80 - 81
Ontario Fire College, Lorne E. McNeice 26 - 33, 45, 47
Hamilton F.D., Capt. Dave Cossette 40T, CF5
Jim Corrigan 48 - 49, 57, 58, 94 - 94, 178T&B
North York F.D. Ron MacQueen, Greg Alexander, Steve
Croft 60 - 61, 67B, 134T, 136-137, 141, 142T&B, 146-
147, 148, 176B, 180B, 132-133
Linda Green 5
Gary (Air) Wignal 66, 67T, 68 - 69, 70T&B, 71, 134B, 135
Gilles Reneaud 73, 75, 76, 78 - 79, 98, 140T, 144, 145,
103, 108, 111, 122, 123
David Youell/Blazing Saddles 74, 118 - 119, 120, CF4
Steve Brabazon 77
Steve Rutledge 84 - 85
Winnipeg Free Press 86 - 87, 90B
Calgary F.D. Orlo Tveter 90T, 92 - 93, 199, 116 - 117
Gordon Lee 100 - 101
Edmonton F.D. Gerry Emas 138, 140B
Stephenville F.D. Robert Betts 139
Windsor Star 142
Origin and Cause 155T&B
Keith Gosse 102
Regina F.D. Grant Nicurity 104 - 105, 109T
Andrew A. Sanojca 106 - 107, 109B
Bombardier Inc., Canadair 158 - 159, 160, 162 - 163

Daryll Schott 161
Paul-Emile Ouellette 164 - 171
David Green 182 - 183
Victoria F.D. Archives 112 - 113
John McQuarrie 196BL
Vic Schertou 114 - 115
Mike Sharpe 128
Eric Hodgkinson 129
Doug Diet CF1
Mike McNulty CF2

Acknowledgements

I wasn't sure I'd ever get to the day when this labour of love was put to bed. So many have been instrumental in it I'm not too sure where to start. I guess the beginning is a good place. To Bill Schorse for his patience when answering a young man's questions, Fred Wynn for honing the raw skills, Larry Wilson for 'all right is all wrong' unless spelled as two words, Betty Whittington for the editing and the wine, Frank McDonald for his constant encouragement, R. Alan Harris, Greg Harris, Paul Lebreux and Sal Bevan for just believing in the project, my mother for giving me tenacity, my big brother Jim for the star to follow and my wonderful wife Linda who stood behind me as I chased my dreams.

The generous assistance of Fire Prevention Canada most notably directors Don Moreau, Terry Ritchie, Marcel Ethier and Barrie Lough for co-ordination of my cross country run and review of photos, the support of the Canadian Association of Fire Chiefs, the Association of Canadian Fire Marshals and Fire Commissioners, the Canadian Automatic Sprinkler Association and Lorne Campbell of Canadian FireFighter but mostly to my new family. The hundreds of firefighters who answered question after question, who showed me the ropes and the Lion's balls. Without their help this book would not be. To mention all would be an impossibility so if I've missed you in particular chew me out when we next meet. Special thanks to Shawn O'Neil, Dean Taylor, Bob Parent, Bernie Mathison, Al Karkkainen, Bob Rainboth, Chris Whitney, Randy Foster, Dr. Wayne Corneil, Jeff Lee for the outsiders look at the inside and the guts to tell it like it is and Lyal Fraser who started it all. Finally to Dave O'Malley and the crew at Aerographics for their patience with the perfectionist in me and their brilliant design.

One down ...three to go.

Allan de la Plante

CANADIAN
AUTOMATIC
SPRINKLER
ASSOCIATION